# Jungle Jingles
## and other Animal Poems

JUNGLE JINGLES AND OTHER ANIMAL POEMS
A YOUNG CORGI BOOK 978 0 552 56739 8

First published in Great Britain by Doubleday,
an imprint of Random House Children's Publishers UK
A Random House Group Company

Doubleday edition published 1990
Young Corgi edition published 2002

This edition published 2013

1 3 5 7 9 10 8 6 4 2

The Random House Group Limited supports the Forest Stewardship Council® (FSC®), the leading
international forest-certification organisation. Our books carrying the FSC label are printed
on FSC®-certified paper. FSC is the only forest-certification scheme supported by the leading
environmental organisations, including Greenpeace. Our paper procurement policy
can be found at www.randomhouse.co.uk/environment

Set in Palatino

Young Corgi Books are published by Random House Children's Publishers UK,
61–63 Uxbridge Road, London W5 5SA

www.randomhousechildrens.co.uk
www.randomhouse.co.uk

Addresses for companies within The Random House Group Limited
can be found at: www.randomhouse.co.uk/offices.htm

THE RANDOM HOUSE GROUP Limited Reg. No. 954009

A CIP catalogue record for this book is available from the British Library.

Printed and bound in Great Britain by CPI Group (UK) Ltd, Croydon CR0 4YY

# Dick King-Smith

# Jungle Jingles
## and other Animal Poems

Illustrated by Jonathan Allen

YOUNG CORGI

# CONTENTS

Jungle Jingles   2

?!   4

No Wings, No Tail, Two Names   5

In the Soup   6

Tit for Tat   8

Strippers   9

Look Back in Wonder   10

Enough to Make You Sick   12

Splat!   14

Lost for Words   16

Suck it and See   18

His and Hers   19

Take Cover   20

We Have Lift-Off   22

Best Foot Forward   24

Catcall   26

Seaside Suicide 28

Like It or Lump It 30

A Family Picnic 32

Tale of a Tail 34

Fore and Aft 36

Horse Sense 37

Free Ride 38

Hear! Hear! 40

Phew! 42

Fishing Finger 44

A Game of Squash 46

Gulp! 48

Starting from Scratch 49

Jolly Blue Giant 50

Down the Hatch 52

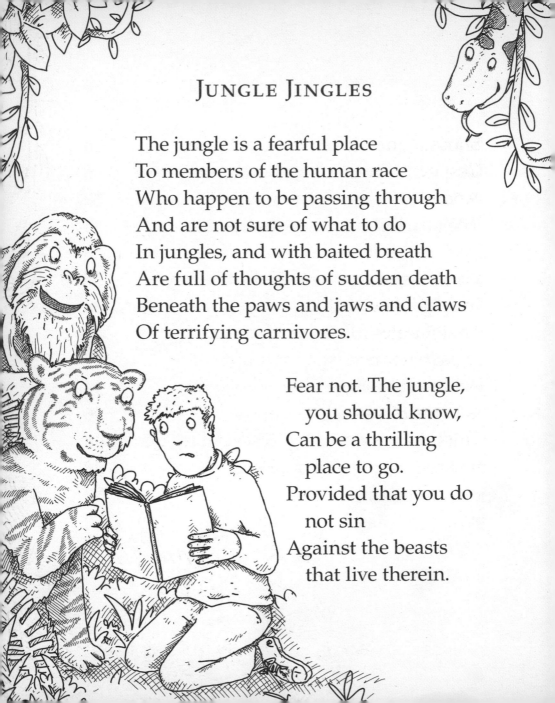

# JUNGLE JINGLES

The jungle is a fearful place
To members of the human race
Who happen to be passing through
And are not sure of what to do
In jungles, and with baited breath
Are full of thoughts of sudden death
Beneath the paws and jaws and claws
Of terrifying carnivores.

Fear not. The jungle,
    you should know,
Can be a thrilling
    place to go.
Provided that you do
    not sin
Against the beasts
    that live therein.

Shoot them with camera, not gun,
Respect them, each and every one,
And never take them unawares –
The jungle isn't yours, it's theirs.

However, should you find some day –
In spite of everything I say –
That jungles fill you with alarm,
A useful way of staying calm
And keeping cool and passing time
Is to recite a little rhyme,
You'll find your fear will soon have gone.
So here are one or two. Read on.

?!

Should you meet a herd of Zebras
And you cannot tell the hebras
Of the Zebras from the shebras –
Watch which way each Zebra peebras.

# No Wings, No Tail, Two Names

The Kiwi's a bird with another appellation –
The Apteryx. And, should you ever chance
  to mention
This spellbinding fact to a friend or a relation,
It's apteryxcite their immediate attention.

# In the Soup

A wagging tail will tell you that
A Dog is overjoyed;
In contradiction to a Cat,
Which wags when it's annoyed.

The Ox's tail, one has to state,
Seems mournfully to droop:
It's just as though it knew its fate –
To end as oxtail soup.

# Tit for Tat

The Anteater has always fed
On Ants, but when at last he's dead,
The Ants will feed on him instead.

# STRIPPERS

If you fall in a river that's full of Piranha,
They'll strip off your flesh like you'd skin
  a banana.
There's no time for screaming, there's no time
  for groans.
In forty-five seconds you're nothing but bones.

# Look Back in Wonder

Though the Elephant's behind
Is delightfully designed,
And the rump of any Rhino's mighty fine,
Though the buttocks of a Bear
Are indubitably fair,
And the Pig is fundamentally divine,
Though the bum of any Bison
Is a singularly nice un,
And the backside of a Boa never stops –
Yet not one's got such a bottom as
The hugeous Hippopotamus.
For bottoms, Hippopotami are tops.

# Enough to Make You Sick

What if every day you ate
Food of twice your body-weight?
That is what the Pygmy Shrew
(Just to stay alive) must do.
Think what it would mean to you.

Seven bucketfuls of chips,
Several dozen Instant Whips,
Twenty packs of Shredded Wheat,
Thirty tins of luncheon meat –
That is what you'd have to eat.

Plus – six chickens, and a ham,
Forty-seven pots of jam,
Fifty bars of Milky Way.
All that in a single day!
'Lovely!' did I hear you say?

Thank your lucky stars that you
Were not born a Pygmy Shrew.

# Splat!

No creature can create it
Or hope to imitate it.
To do this thing no other beast knows how.

However much they practise,
The plain and simple fact is –
No-one can make a cowpat like a Cow.

# Lost for Words

A little whistling note to call its calf.
That is the only noise the tall Giraffe
Can make. Apart from that, it has no choice
But silence, for it doesn't have a voice.
For joy the tall Giraffe can never shout –
Its mouth will open, but no sound comes out.
And if it's sad or wounded or bereaved,
What happens must be seen to be believed,
For silently, out of each liquid eye,
The tears come dropping from the very sky.
Be kindly then, and never never laugh
At that dumb animal, the tall Giraffe.

# SUCK IT AND SEE

The taste of blood, observers note,
Is most appealing to the Stoat,
Which grabs a rabbit by the throat,
And dines upon it, table-d'hôte.

# His and Hers

The Worms are all hermaphrodites.
The consequence of this is
That ev'ry Worm you ever sight's
A Mr and a Mrs.

# Take Cover

The Vulture feeds on the deceased
Of absolutely ev'ry beast.
It isn't fussy in the least
And any body makes a feast.

All corpses serve to appetize
And none escapes the Vulture's eyes.
As soon as any creature dies,
Down drops the Vulture from the skies.

Remember then – before you're dead –
It's better if you die in bed
Or even in the garden shed
If there are Vultures overhead.

# We Have Lift-Off

Young Gannets like practising flying
In their nests on the high narrow ledges.
The impetuous things
Keep on flapping their wings
While perched on the ultimate edges.

But all of the time that they're trying,
They are fearful of premature motion.
So they're careful to stand
Facing in towards land
And keeping their backs to the ocean.

# BEST FOOT FORWARD

You thought the Centipede possessed
Exactly fifty pairs of feet?
Is that the figure you'd have guessed?
The answer isn't quite so neat.

For scientific men who've seen
Each centipedal cousin,
Find some have only got fifteen
And some have fifteen dozen.

# CATCALL

The Puma (or the Mountain Lion
Or Cougar or the Catamount)
May have no need of that amount
Of labels to rely on.

But when he fancies lambs to eat
All farmers curse him till they're hoarse.
They call the Puma names too coarse
And vulgar to repeat.

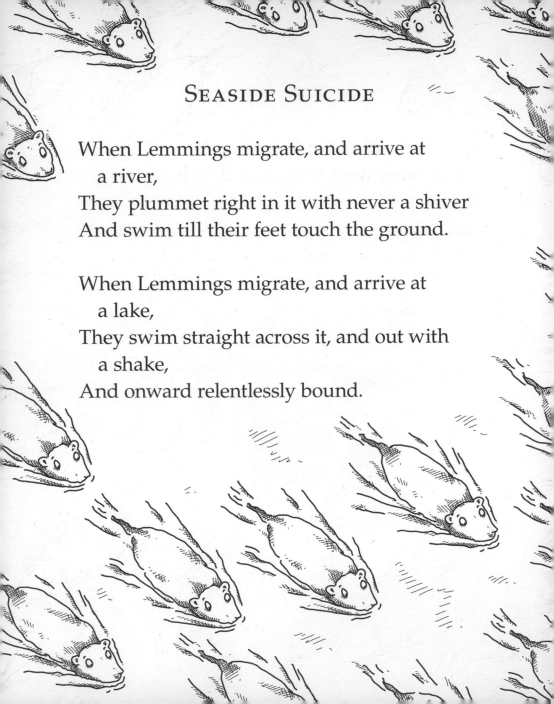

# SEASIDE SUICIDE

When Lemmings migrate, and arrive at
 a river,
They plummet right in it with never a shiver
And swim till their feet touch the ground.

When Lemmings migrate, and arrive at
 a lake,
They swim straight across it, and out with
 a shake,
And onward relentlessly bound.

And then, when the Lemmings'
  migratory host
Has crossed the whole land and arrived at
  the coast,
They swim out to sea and are drowned.

# Like It or Lump It

The Camel sports a brace of humps,
The Dromedary only one.
It looks as though it's in the dumps
And never having any fun.
The reason, so the experts tell us,
Is that the Dromedary's jealous.

# A FAMILY PICNIC

If you meet with a man-eating Tiger,
Don't think that it only eats men.
When it's polished off Dad, it'll start on your
    mother,
Your sister, your auntie, your new baby
    brother,
And shortly be hungry again.

For afters, it might manage you and your gran,
So don't think a man-eater only eats man.

# TALE OF A TAIL

The Boodie is a quarter-size
Relation of the Kangaroo.
You hardly would believe your eyes
When witnessing what Boodies do
To make their nests. Each picks up straw
And puts it on its hairy tail
Which curls around, to squeeze it more
And more, and make a little bale.

Salute the Boodie, tail compactly curled!
First-ever pick-up baler in the world!

# FORE AND AFT

The Mole, which tunnels very well,
Can find its way by touch and smell:
The many bristles on its nose
Send messages as down it goes.
And though it's practically blind,
It has a sensitive behind –
Just one of Nature's many mercies
And useful when the Mole reverses.

# Horse Sense

The Suffolk Punch eats grass for lunch
In spring and summer – that's to say,
In winter it is fed on hay.
There is a difference of course
From any lesser breed of horse –
The Suffolk Punch eats twice as munch.

# FREE RIDE

When the babies of the Crocodile
Hatch out beside the River Nile,
And first emerge upon its sandy shores,
She transports her sons and daughters

To the safety of its waters,
Holding all of them within her mighty jaws.
See how tenderly she holds her little crew!
(But I shouldn't let her try it on with you.)

# HEAR! HEAR!

Though you may feel a little fear
If there's an Earwig in your ear,
There is no cause for utter dread –
It can't get right inside your head.

But on the whole it might be best
To shift the creature, lest it nest.
An ear that's used for Earwig-rearing
Could cause you partial loss of hearing.

# Phew!

There's nothing on earth that's ever stunk
As bad as a squirt from an angry Skunk.
There's nothing as foul and nothing as
    strong –
A squirt from a Skunk is the world's worst
    pong.

You must leave your house, and you can't
    return
Till they've fumigated it, while you burn
The furnishings and your clothes as well.
You stand there naked and still you smell.

I'll give you a tip (and this is true):
If an angry Skunk ever squirts on you,
The only thing that's of any use
Is a long cold bath in tomato juice.

# FISHING FINGER

The Aye-Aye has a finger that's
  meticulously planned.
It's quite unlike the other fingers
  on the Aye-Aye's hand.
It's long and strong and bony and it's
  very very thin,
And when he finds a beetle's hole,
  the Aye-Aye sticks it in,

Unbends it and extends it and then
  wiggles it about,
And pulls a lot of lovely squashy
  beetle-larvae out.
Which only goes to demonstrate
  what any Aye-Aye knew –
That all these little lemurs have a
  very high I.Q.

# A Game of Squash

If there's one thing that's worse than a
   Headlouse,
Then it must, I suppose, be a Bedlouse.
But as I've understood lice
(And excepting the Woodlice),
Why, the only good louse is a dead louse.

# GULP!

The Pike has one abiding wish –
To swallow any other fish.
It isn't fussy, doesn't mind
What sort, but gobbles any kind.
In fact, it's guaranteed to like
The chance to eat another Pike.

# STARTING FROM SCRATCH

Have you ever been bird-spotting
And observed a Starling squatting
On an ants' nest, and you wonder
As you watch it, why in thunder
Is the silly creature doing
Something it must soon be rueing?
I'll explain.

Parasites that drive it frantic
Make the bird perform this antic,
Knowing ants will then infest it
And efficiently divest it
Of the pests, with formic acid,
Rendering the Starling placid
Once again.

# Jolly Blue Giant

The Blue's the biggest kind of Whale
At thirty metres, top to tail.
The largest creature on the earth
(It's seven metres long at birth!)
And as for weight, it's twenty-five
Times any elephant alive.
If you should meet one face to face,
You need not swim away apace
In fear, or even show alarm,
The Blue won't do you any harm.
It isn't that Blue Whales are wimps.
It's just that all they eat is shrimps.

# DOWN THE HATCH

The Python can unlock its jaws
To gape as wide as double doors,
And then the snake expands its throat
And swallows whole a nanny-goat
Or pig or antelope or sheep,
And goes contentedly to sleep,

Its middle one enormous bulge,
The shape of which does not divulge
What wretched animal has died.
Let's hope it's never you inside
The Python. If it were, my friend,
That, without doubt, would be

THE END

# ❖ ABOUT THE AUTHOR ❖

DICK KING-SMITH was a Gloucestershire farmer until the age of 45, when he gave up farming to become a primary school teacher. His first book, *The Fox Busters*, was published in 1978, and he went on to become a prolific and bestselling full-time author, writing well over a hundred books. His work received many awards, including a Smarties Prize Bronze Medal for *All Because of Jackson* and the Children's Book Award for *Harriet's Hare*, and he was also voted Children's Author of the Year in 1992. His top-selling title *The Sheep-Pig* was developed into the Academy Award nominated movie *Babe*. He passed away in 2011 at the age of 88.

# ❖ THE ADVENTUROUS SNAIL ❖

Snail on board!

Siegfried loves to explore. One day his explorations
take him on a big adventure – from his home in the
grass, to the airport, on to an aeroplane and
all the way to America!

There he makes some very important friends,
Mr Ambassador and Mr President, finds a new
home in a sandwich box – and also meets
the lovely Peggy Sue . . .

978 0 552 56741 1

# 🐾 TITUS RULES OK 🐾

"Titus, my boy," said the Queen, "I have a funny feeling that you are going to be a very special dog."

Titus is a young corgi puppy, growing up in Windsor Castle. There is lots he must learn (like how not to trip up Prince Philip!). Soon he becomes the Queen's favourite, and she even lets him sleep on her bed at night! And it is because of Titus that Her Majesty finally does something very surprising . . .

978 0 552 55431 2